GEMARAKUP Super Sleuth 3

LOST ON SKULL MOUNTAIN

by Miriam Stark Zakon

Tamar Books

FIRST EDITION
First Impression . . . May 1994

Published and Distributed by
MESORAH PUBLICATIONS, Ltd.
4401 Second Avenue
Brooklyn, New York 11232

Distributed in Europe by
J. LEHMANN HEBREW BOOKSELLERS
20 Cambridge Terrace
Gateshead, Tyne and Wear
England NE8 1RP

Distributed in Israel by
SIFRIATI / A. GITLER – BOOKS
4 Bilu Street
P.O.B. 14075
Tel Aviv 61140

Distributed in Australia & New Zealand by
GOLD'S BOOK & GIFT CO.
36 William Street
Balaclava 3183, Vic., Australia

Distributed in South Africa by
KOLLEL BOOKSHOP
22 Muller Street
Yeoville 2198, Johannesburg, South Africa

Manufactured in the United States of America by Noble Book Press Corp.

Table of Contents

I.
Lost On Skull Mountain!
A Gemarakup Mini-Adventure

Attention Camp Kayitz campers. Attention Camp Kayitz campers. Prepare for an incredible *Rosh Chodesh* treat."

Sitting on his bunk in a corner of a large wood-paneled room, Yisrael David Finkel — also known as Gemarakup — gave a wry grin. An incredible treat? Right. Maybe jelly donuts for dessert, or a walk down the road to see the bungalow colonies. After a week in camp, he'd noticed that words like incredible, unbelievable, and amazing were used to describe just about everything. Incredible? Big deal.

The tinny voice crackled on. "Right after *davening*, breakfast, and *shiur*, bunks *aleph* through *yud* will be traveling to Kiddyland!"

Gemarakup could hear ragged cheers and shouting coming from the direction of the younger bunks as the children got the news that they would be going to the popular amusement park.

"Bunks *yud* and up will be taking a full-day hike . . . up Skull Mountain!"

Gemarakup sat up and almost bumped his head on the low ceiling. Well, this really *was* a treat!

Through the small, dust-encrusted window that was next to his bunk bed, Gemarakup could see a distant mountain range covered with fir trees standing motionless in the clear air. The tallest peak, rising starkly into the cloudless blue sky, was known, rather ominously, as Skull Mountain.

The intercom went on relentlessly. "So get out your mountain-climbing equipment, explorers, and prepare for adventure!"

Gemarakup bounced quickly out of bed and joined his bunkmates, who were milling eagerly around their counselor. "What should we take? What do we need?" Dovid Miller asked excitedly.

Their counselor, Yossi, scratched his bristly red hair, thought for a moment, then spoke. "Canteens. Fill up bottles and canteens with water. Camp will send food, but *nosh* always comes in handy." He gave an engaging grin. "Wear good sneakers and old pants — you'll probably tear them anyway, climbing up the mountain. Caps against the sun. Cameras, of course. That should be more than enough to take along," he ended, turning to his own shelf and gathering up his things.

"Enough for him, maybe," Gemarakup heard a voice mutter. He turned towards the voice. Baruch Glickstein.

It figured. Baruch Glickstein was a newcomer to Camp Kayitz, but everybody already knew him. How could you not know the kid who drove up in a Lincoln when everybody else came up on the camp bus? How could you not notice the boy with the professional snorkeling equipment, particularly when he made sure to mention that it had cost more than two hundred dollars? Glickstein was the rich boy with the notebook computer he wouldn't share, the Reebok sneakers too fancy to kick a ball with, and the cellular phone that the head counselor had banned on camp grounds. And now, it seemed, the very proud owner of a professional mountain-climbing kit.

"It's a small Alpine survival pack," Baruch explained — bragged might be a better word — to Gemarakup. "It's got a Swiss army knife. Nylon cord. Matches in a waterproof bag. Compass. First-aid kit. Everything you might need if you get stuck. And all the best quality, of course!"

"Of course," Gemarakup muttered. It was no sin to be wealthy, Gemarakup mused as he walked away, but when you combined riches with a personality like Glickstein's, the combination was annoying.

The "annoying combination" seemed destined to stalk Gemarakup throughout the day. For some reason, Baruch decided to stick as close to Gemarakup as the moss which clung to the rocks that they climbed. While Gemarakup tried to appreciate the wonders of *Hashem's* natural world, he was forced to listen to the wonders of Baruch's compact disc player. A bubbling brook reminded Baruch of his jacuzzi back home; no wildflowers could match his father's carefully cultivated rose garden; the breathtaking scenery couldn't compare with what Baruch had seen during his trip to Switzerland.

With a small part of his brain Gemarakup listened, nodded and made curt replies; the rest of him concentrated on going up the snaky, treacherous path without falling, while enjoying the incredibly beautiful scenery that surrounded him.

Maybe it was Gemarakup's fast pace, as he desperately tried to outrace his braggart companion. Perhaps it was Baruch's top-of-the-line Reebok climbing shoes (one of six pairs of sports shoes that he'd brought in his oversized trunk) that allowed him to set a grueling pace. Whatever the reason, the pair led the group of climbers throughout the day, and proudly reached the narrow summit of Skull Mountain first, well ahead of the others.

The boys grinned at each other and held their fists aloft in triumph. Gemarakup felt a rush of good feeling go through him as he looked at his sweaty, dusty companion. The last hour had been the most grueling of the climb and they had walked in silent concentration. Even Baruch couldn't brag under such circumstances which may explain why Gemarakup could look so kindly upon his climbing companion.

"We made it!" Baruch exclaimed.

"Yeah. Good job," Gemarakup said. "So what do we do now?"

"Now? We wait for the others to catch up. And we do what all mountain climbers do."

"What's that?" Gemarakup asked, curious.

"We plant our flag!" With a laugh, Baruch grabbed a long branch that had fallen from a fine old oak tree nearby. He took out a large white handkerchief from his pants pocket, and, using the scissors from his Alpine survival kit, carefully cut a small hole in the corner. Then he stuck the branch through the hole and proudly waved his makeshift flag.

"Wait a minute," said Gemarakup, laughing. "It's not done yet."

He took a black marker out of his pocket, put the handkerchief down on a flat rock, and quickly wrote something.

"What's it say?" Baruch asked.

"Let's keep it simple: BARUCH AND GEMARAKUP WERE HERE," his friend answered.

They stuck the branch into the hard ground, surrounded it with small rocks to keep it upright, and, with sighs of satisfaction, watched their "flag" wave proudly in the quickening breeze.

A few minutes passed. The boys sat on the ground, resting. They could hear the sound of the other boys making their noisy way up the mountain, grunting and shouting with the effort of the climb.

"Have some peanuts," Baruch offered, searching through his bag. "They're honey-roasted, gourmet — the best on the market."

Gemarakup sighed. He felt all his good feelings dissipate as he anticipated another onslaught of bragging.

He jumped to his feet. "I'm going to explore a little," he said, hoping to get away from Baruch's incessant boasts.

No luck. Baruch snapped his backpack shut and joined him. The two made their way carefully down a steep dirt track that led away from the summit towards the other side of the mountain.

"We shouldn't go too far," Baruch cautioned. Gemarakup hardly heard him. He was lost in a wonderland of thick, gnarled trees and strange boulders. The late midday sun cast weird shadows, giving a mysterious feel to the scene. Now he really felt like an explorer!

He saw a chink between two large rocks. A cave!

"You got a flashlight in that pack of yours?" he asked Baruch, who had followed him through the thick woods, silent for once.

"Sure. With two rechargeable battery packs and a glow-in-the-dark handle," Baruch answered. "Are we . . . going in?" he added, somewhat warily.

"Let's get a little use out of your Alpine kit," Gemarakup answered, bending low to avoid bumping his head on the overhanging rocks.

For a few moments the two walked in a crouched position through the deep darkness. This was no small cave, Gemarakup saw — this was a full-blown tunnel leading . . . where? With thoughts of great explorers racing through his head, Gemarakup forged ahead.

"Are you sure we should be doing this?" Baruch asked.

"Look, I know exactly how to get back. We just turn around and retrace our steps. Don't worry."

"Okay, Gemarakup. It's your show."

Farther and farther they hiked. The walls grew higher; they could stand upright now. As he played the flashlight on the sides of the tunnel, Gemarakup could see rivulets of water sliding slowly down. "I'll bet we're under that brook we passed," he said. The echo of his voice sounded eerie. Suddenly, the tunnel seemed lonely, quiet, and rather menacing. Being an explorer didn't seem quite as much fun as all that. Gemarakup missed his friends — and the friendly rays of the sun.

"Time to turn back," he whispered, trying to avoid the sinister echo.

The two boys turned and marched quickly back in the direction they had come from. Time passed. Baruch looked at his Swiss chronometer watch with its phosphorescent clock face.

"Gemarakup?"

"Yeah?"

"We're walking an awful long time. Shouldn't we have been out of the cave by now?"

Gemarakup fought down a surge of nervousness. "Don't worry, Baruch. We're walking in the right direction. It just seems long."

But watches — particularly Swiss chronometers — don't lie. Another five minutes passed, and another. Finally, Gemarakup had to accept the inescapable fact.

"There must have been a turnoff that we missed in the dark," he said quietly.

"Does that mean . . ."

"We're lost? Yeah, I guess so." Gemarakup forced a laugh. "Now we're really explorers. But don't worry, we'll find our way out."

Both boys silently plodded on. It was cool in the damp tunnel, but beads of sweat appeared on their brows.

Finally, Gemarakup gave a shout that echoed on endlessly. "Look! Up ahead! I see light!"

Baruch Hashem! The two quickened their pace and minutes later found themselves out of the cave. They blinked in the sunshine and looked around them. And saw that, wherever they were — they had never been there before.

They were lost. Hopelessly lost on Skull Mountain.

The next few hours passed like a dream, a bad dream, a horrifying nightmare. On and on they walked, climbed, scrambled, and waded. The sun, together with their spirits, sank lower and lower. Baruch said little, content to follow Gemarakup as he searched frantically and fruitlessly for the trail that had led them up the mountain.

Finally, exhausted, the two sank down on the cool grass.

"It's . . . it's going to be dark soon," Gemarakup said, his voice quivering.

Baruch pulled his pack off his back. "At least we've got the flashlight," he said, trying to sound cheerful.

But cheerfulness was the last thing Gemarakup was interested in. He'd had enough. Enough climbing. Enough exploring. And more than enough of Baruch's bragging!

"Forget about your stupid flashlight, and your whole stupid survival kit!" he shouted, his voice as rough as the pebbles beneath him. "All your dumb, rich boy's gadgets that you've bragged about won't help us one bit!"

The minute the words were out of his mouth Gemarakup regretted them. He remembered the good feelings he'd had when they'd reached the summit together. He remembered how Baruch hadn't complained since they'd gotten into this mess. And he remembered just *who* had gotten them into it: the big shot smart boy, the genius, the one who was always right. Gemarakup.

But regretted words don't disappear. Baruch's face paled; his eyes looked stricken.

"I . . . I didn't mean to brag," he said. "I'm new here in camp. I thought you guys would respect and like me if I showed you the kind of stuff I've got. Everybody knows each other, everybody's friends — I wanted to be part of the crowd too."

Gemarakup thought back to the first days of camp. In the excitement of seeing old friends again, had they been unfriendly to the new kid? And — to be perfectly honest here in the scary darkness of Skull Mountain — were they just a little bit jealous of the boy who'd driven up in a Lincoln?

He shook his head sadly and held out a dirty hand. "Baruch, I'm sorry. We were all out of line. Do you forgive me?"

"Sure, I forgive you."

Well, that was settled. Gemarakup suspected that Baruch's bragging would come to an end; he knew for sure that he would do his best to include him in his crowd of friends.

Now to problem number two.

How in the world to get out of here?

Darkness settled on the two huddled figures. Baruch managed a wry smile. "Some *Rosh Chodesh* treat, huh?"

Gemarakup was almost too disheartened to answer. But while his body drooped, his mind went into gear. Almost against his will, he thought about their plight. Something in Baruch's words . . . something . . .

Lost on Skull Mountain! / 13

Suddenly he jumped up, all fatigue gone. "Baruch, I owe you another apology — and a thanks! I was wrong about your Alpine pack — it *will* come in handy. It's going to save us!"

Do we let our heroes spend a scary night on Skull Mountain — or do we rescue them? Think hard and fast (it's cold up there!) — and turn to page 70 for the solution.

II.

The Momentous Mystery
of the Missing Money
Featuring Tamar
Kid Detective

Part 1

 door burst open in the Finkel home.

"Did you hear about that strange new *minhag*?" Gemarakup asked, a trace of irritation in his usually pleasant voice. "It's called knocking before you come into someone's room."

Gemarakup's nine-year-old sister, Tamar, looked contrite. "Sorry," she said, "but it was an emergency. I've got these math problems, see, and Mrs. Pilner is going to kill me if I don't get them done for tomorrow, and I haven't the slightest idea . . . Gemarakup! What's that?" she ended with a shriek.

"That," her brother explained coolly, "is the money that I've earned this week."

"Just this week!" Tamar looked at the stacks of ten-, five-, and one-dollar bills, the quarters, dimes, and nickels, all carefully piled up on her brother's desk. "That's a fortune! You must have about a hundred dollars there!"

Gemarakup eyed her wearily. "Forty-three dollars and twenty-nine cents, to be exact," he said.

Tamar's eyes widened. All that money — in just one week! "What'd you do, rob a bank?" she demanded with a grin.

Her brother condescended to return the smile. "Not exactly, Tamar. I simply became an entrepreneur."

"Entrepe-what?"

"A businessman, looking for opportunities to make some cool cash." Gemarakup pointed to a pile of dimes. "I sold *nosh* after school to the kids. That's my profit over there. I washed cars" — he indicated the quarters, "and that's what I got from it. I've worked really hard these past few days. I made five dollars from Mr. Mandel for mowing his lawn, and ten bucks babysitting for the Miller kids."

Tamar stared at her brother, open-mouthed. She hadn't seen him around much lately, but she had assumed he'd been busy with tests and reports. It had never occurred to her that he'd become an entrop . . . entrip . . . a big businessman!

"What in the world are you collecting so much money for?" she asked, after a moment's silence.

"You remember how Abba said we can't use the computer anymore?" Gemarakup said.

Tamar nodded. Sure she remembered. Gemarakup and his best friend, Slugger, had caught "computer fever" over the past few weeks, spending all their spare time playing Tetris, Xonix, Commander Keene and half a dozen other great games. Until the Finkel's keyboard, under the onslaught of two over-enthusiastic players, began to stick and Abba had declared the computer off-limits. The result of the ban had been one presumably relieved computer — and two very sulky sixth graders.

"But you can't buy yourself a computer with only forty-three dollars . . ." Tamar protested.

" . . . and twenty-nine cents," her brother laughed. "Of course not. But ninety-nine dollars will get you a special computer game keypad and joystick, together with a whole stock of great new games!" Gemarakup's eyes glowed with anticipation. "Abba was just mad because we spoiled his keyboard — but with the keypad we can play what we want, and not bother him at all!"

"Uh, speaking of not bothering . . ." Tamar said hesitantly, "what about my math problems? Or are you charging for tutoring too?"

Gemarakup's eyes lit up for a moment. No, it just wouldn't do. He sighed. "Okay kid, get out your book and let's take a look." He glanced at his watch. "But make it quick. I'm babysitting tonight."

Tamar bowed low. "Certainly, Baron Rothschild," she said gravely. Then she smiled. "And speaking of Rothschild, today in school I heard a great story for your collection, about the first Baron and how he got wealthy."

Gemarakup waved her off. "Look, Tamar, I'll give you a hand with the homework, but that's enough. I really have to go out and earn some more dough. And I've heard all those Rothschild stories already."

Tamar sighed. Her brother always, but always, loved a good story, even if he'd heard it before. Collecting tales of *gedolim* was his special hobby. But now it seemed that he was more interested in collecting money.

With a grim look, she turned to her math.

Tamar's struggle with fractions (how much was 3/8 times 1/3 anyway?) was interrupted by the sound of the doorbell. Moments later she heard her mother call. "Yisrael David. Tamar Rachel. Get down here. Now."

Tamar and Gemarakup exchanged glances. They recognized that tone. That was Imma's no-nonsense, someone-did-some-thing-awful-and-is-about-to-get-it voice. Their thoughts raced as their feet fled down the stairs. No one had left a turtle on the stairs, run a bubble bath with a package of laundry detergent, or forgotten an ice-cream cone on Imma's favorite lounge chair.

Mrs. Finkel stood in her kitchen surrounded by evidence of one of her periodic baking binges: food processor parts and measuring cups and egg beaters all piled up in the sink; bowl after bowl sticky with chocolate batter and lemon icing and meringues; cookbooks piled up one on the other; rolling pins and cookie cutters and cracked egg shells. Tamar and Gemarakup noticed three large brown bags covering one corner of the countertop.

But instead of the usual smiling face awaiting volunteers to lick the bowls and the beaters, they saw a pair of icy eyes.

"What's wrong, Imma?" Gemarakup asked quietly.

Mrs. Finkel favored the two of them with a frosty stare. "Have either of you taken twenty dollars from the kitchen?" she asked quietly.

Tamar stared, perplexed. "Huh?"

"Before he left for learning, Abba gave me two ten-dollar bills to pay the butcher when he made his delivery. I put them on the counter. The butcher just came — and when I went to pay him, I found that both bills were gone! I gave him a check instead, and now I want to know — who took that money?" She gave

the two of them a withering look. "No one has been in or out of the kitchen except for us. So," she ended quietly, "who took the money without permission?"

Tamar was vociferous in her denials. "I didn't, Imma! I was doing my homework all night! I didn't even come into the kitchen!"

"That's right, doll, you didn't," her mother said. She turned an accusing gaze towards her eldest son. "You've been trying to earn money these past few days, haven't you, Yisrael?"

"Yeah, Imma, but . . ."

"And you were in the kitchen tonight, weren't you?" the voice went on relentlessly.

"Yeah, Imma, I came down for a drink, but . . ."

"Are you sure, absolutely sure, that you didn't . . . didn't see the money and maybe forget yourself." The reproachful voice took on a different, more pleading tone. "Please be mature and admit if you did the wrong thing."

Gemarakup, his cheeks scarlet, wordlessly turned around and raced up the stairs. Moments later, he handed over two ten-dollar bills to his moist-eyed mother.

"I'm sorry, Imma. I really am."

With that, he bowed to Tamar, who had watched the scene in disbelief. "Baron Rothschild, at your service," he said bitterly.

Tamar stared at her brother. Gemarakup . . . a thief? Impossible! But he'd confessed! Or . . . had he?

"Wait a minute!" she cried. "Gemarakup didn't take that money! And I can prove it!"

How does Tamar know her brother is honest? Turn to page 71 for the solution.

III.

The Momentous Mystery
of the Missing Money

Part 2

hree baffled Finkels sat glumly around a cluttered kitchen table.

"Gemarakup didn't take it," Tamar said for the tenth time.

"You proved that nicely," her mother answered, rewarding her with a warm and grateful look.

"I didn't take it," Tamar continued her endless recital.

"You weren't in the kitchen the entire night," Gemarakup agreed.

"And Imma didn't take it," Tamar went on.

"No, I think we can rule that out," her mother said dryly.

"So — if Gemarakup didn't take it, and if I didn't take it, and if Imma didn't take it — then who *did* take the money?"

Just a few hours ago, Mr. Finkel had left twenty dollars on the kitchen counter for his wife. No one but the three Finkels had been in the kitchen since then — and yet now the money was gone!

Mrs. Finkel gave a small smile. "Look, kids, the main thing is that we're all honest — and, *baruch Hashem*, no one's suspecting anyone else falsely. It's just not worth getting all excited about money."

"It's not the twenty dollars," Gemarakup explained. "I just want to know how in the world the money disappeared. I hate not knowing things. I won't be able to sleep all night, trying to figure this one out."

"I know, sweetie, but remember, there's lots of things you don't know and you sleep just fine anyway. You don't know who your teacher will be next year. You don't know who you'll marry — and how the *shidduch* will come about. You don't even know if tomorrow will be rainy or not!"

"I don't know fractions," Tamar added pensively, "and I've never lost any sleep over it. As a matter of fact," she laughed, "nothing puts me to sleep better than a bunch of math problems!"

Gemarakup looked unconvinced. His mother stood up. "One thing I do know," she said briskly.

"What's that, Imma?"

"I know who's going to help me clean up this kitchen," she said, casting a rueful glance at the mess surrounding her.

But as they washed utensils, licked bowls, wiped counters, and carefully stacked up cookbooks, Gemarakup couldn't help himself from thinking about the mysterious person who had somehow managed to enter, steal, and vanish into the unknown without leaving a trace. "Who cares who I'll marry, and how the *shidduch* will come about?" he thought impatiently. "I want to know who the thief is!"

Suddenly, he leaped up and gave a shout. "*Shidduch*! That's it!" He turned to his mother and sister, who were looking at him as though he'd gone mad. "I know who the thief was — and where to find the money!" he yelled.

Can you guess where the money is? Turn to page 74 for the solution.

IV.

Cracking the Case of the Card Collection

irst, it had been marbles. For three weeks, you couldn't walk through the second grade classroom of Yeshivah Ahavas Chesed without stepping and slipping on red, green, blue, and yellow marbles that had rolled out of their owners' bags. You could win 'em, trade 'em, or beg your best friend to loan you a few.

And then, as suddenly as they'd appeared, the marbles were gone, vanished like the frogs in Egypt after the plague was over.

The marbles were swiftly followed by glow-in-the-dark stickers, which were followed by animal-shaped erasers, which were followed by foreign stamps and coins.

Gemarakup had never seen a class so addicted to fads and collections. He had watched, amused, as the craze for foreign stamps began to pall. He had wondered, rather condescendingly, what would come next.

And then he'd found out.

"I can't believe it!" Gemarakup moaned to his friend, Slugger. "Of all the rotten luck! That nutty second grade has gotten into *Rebbe* cards!"

Slugger, who was busy gazing at a hero sandwich that he'd created the night before, and wondering how in the world one ate a salami-baloney-pastrami with mustard, lettuce, pickles and tomatoes on French bread, wasn't terribly impressed by his friend's complaint. "So what? You've been collecting *Rebbe* cards for years. Why should they be different from you?"

"Different? Of course it's different," Gemarakup exploded.

"Why?" asked Slugger, who had by now decided that the human mouth simply could not accommodate his work of art and so was carefully dismantling his sandwich.

"I'll tell you why, if you quit playing with your lunch," Gemarakup answered testily. He marked each point on his fingers. "One — I've been collecting cards for years, and will be collecting for years to come. You know the second grade — two weeks from now they'll be interested in left-footed sneakers or something equally crazy. Two — I don't only collect *Rebbe* cards. I collect the stories of the *Rebbes*, which is a lot more important."

"Okay, okay, you're different. But I still don't see why you're so upset about it. It's only a fad. Are you scared of the competition? Think they'll drive the price of cards up?"

Gemarakup glared at his friend, who was cheerfully munching a pickle. "No, I am *not* scared of the competition. But everyone in school knows about my collection. Now that the second grade has decided that *Rebbe* cards are 'in,' I'll never have a minute free. I've already had three kids come to me at recess to beg me to lend them some Steiplers. Two of them met me after school, asking for the privilege of seeing my albums. And one little monster offered to trade his brother's new bike for a Maharal of Prague!"

"Did you take the little *golem* up on his offer?" asked Slugger, laughing uproariously at his own joke.

"It's not funny! I'm the official expert on *Rebbe* cards, and they're not going to give me a minute's peace! Life is going to be impossible the next few days!"

"Look at the bright side," Slugger advised his friend. "If you're so important — maybe they'll start trading pictures of you!"

If life didn't get impossible, it certainly wasn't terribly pleasant. Recess found Gemarakup wearing a hunted look as he strove to stay out of the second graders' way. Everyone in the class, it seemed, wanted to know which cards were rarest or how to get a certain *gadol*.

But it wasn't until after school on Friday afternoon that Gemarakup really saw how difficult it was to be the "*rebbe* of the *Rebbe* cards."

He had just finished packing up his backpack when four second graders raced into his classroom, looking distressed and angry.

"Gemarakup, we need your help!" one of them, a freckled redhead by the name of Levi Cohen, announced.

Gemarakup sighed. "What's the problem?" he asked, resigned.

"Yehoshua Schwartzman and Dovid Bergman! They're ready to kill each other!" came the answer.

Gemarakup continued to put his *sefarim* neatly in his pack. Somehow, murder in the second grade seemed an unlikely prospect. "Why?" he asked mildly.

"It's like this," redheaded Levi explained. "Yehoshua, see, he's got this great collection of *Rebbe* cards. And Dovid also has a lot of them. They're the two biggest collectors in the class."

Gemarakup nodded. He'd met both boys. Nice kids, if a little crazy on the subject of collecting.

"So this morning, on the way to school, I found this."

Gemarakup looked with interest at the object that Levi held out. It was a small plastic bag filled with — of course — *Rebbe* cards.

"It was right next to our classroom," Levi continued.

"Must have fallen out of someone's backpack," Gemarakup murmured.

"That's right. And Yehoshua claims that the cards are his! And Dovid says they're his! And they're going to kill each other! And maybe me!"

"Where are they now?" Gemarakup asked, interested despite himself.

"Out in the schoolyard, yelling at each other."

"Okay, let's go."

In the yard Gemarakup found that Levi was just a little in error. The two competitors were no longer hurling insults; they were too busy wrestling each other to the ground.

"Okay, break it up!" Gemarakup commanded. The small group of second graders that had gathered around them gave a collective sigh of relief. A sixth grader would know what to do.

Within minutes, Gemarakup had separated the two. He looked at the sullen boys standing on each side.

"The cards are mine!" shouted Yehoshua, once he'd gotten his breath back. "Give them to me," he added, making a fierce gesture in Levi's direction.

"Don't you dare!" warned Dovid. "They're mine!"

Gemarakup thought deeply for a minute. "There's about twenty cards here," he said. "Why don't you just split them between you?"

"Will not!" Dovid said heatedly. "Why should I give my cards to him?"

Yehoshua just contented himself with sticking out his tongue.

Gemarakup sighed. Obviously, his *Shlomo HaMelech*-like gesture wasn't going to work.

He pointed to the cards. "Let me see them. Maybe there's a clue."

Slowly he fingered each one. A Chofetz Chaim, a Gerrer *Rebbe*, *Rav* Elchanan Wasserman. Ridiculous to be fighting over such *tzaddikim,* but then again, Gemarakup thought, who could expect sense from two furious seven-year-olds?

Feeling increasingly helpless, he continued to sift through the pile, looking for some sort of clue to the ownership. *Rav* Moshe Feinstein, the Chazon Ish, the *Rav* of Lodz.

Wait! That was it!

Excitedly, he turned to the expectant group surrounding him. "Boys, it's *erev Shabbos* — time to get home. The show's over. And you two," he said, turning to Dovid and Yehoshua, "come with me."

"But who gets the cards?" Levi asked.

"Don't worry about it," Gemarakup answered. "I'll take care of it."

With that, he turned on his heel, followed by two puzzled boys.

How will Gemarakup figure out who gets the cards? For the solution, turn to page 77.

V.
When Is a Painter
Not a Painter?

emarakup and his friend Slugger were indeed slugging it out. No, it wasn't a baseball game or a boxing match — the two friends were wrangling together over a particularly difficult *sugya* in *Gemara*.

And things weren't going well. Not at all.

For the fifth time, the two boys read the words, trying to make sense of them. No use. They simply couldn't make heads or tails of what the *Tanna* was trying to say.

"Tamar, I'm trying to concentrate," Gemarakup said irritably to his sister, who was ensconced on the couch nearby, absorbed in a book. "Please stop that."

"Stop what?"

"Crunching that apple like that. The sound is driving me crazy."

Tamar giggled. "Come off it, Gemarakup. It's your brains that are the problem — not my apple."

"Well, it's impossible to concentrate in here," Gemarakup answered defensively. "Between apple-munching sisters and the smell of paint, who can think clearly?"

"I thought I smelled turpentine," Slugger said. "What's up?"

"My mom couldn't stand the sight of our dirty walls anymore so she's brought in someone to paint. It's been like this all week. He'll be coming in to do the study next."

As if on cue, an apparition in paint-smeared blue overalls came into the room, dragging an equally paint-smeared wooden ladder behind him.

"Hi, kids," the painter said cheerfully as he made a second trip to carry in his buckets and brushes. "Wanna watch?"

Gemarakup barely glanced up. "No, we're learning," he announced importantly. He closed his *sefer* with a bang and turned to Slugger. "Come on, let's go somewhere where we can get some help. This is too hard a *sugya* to handle ourselves."

From high atop his ladder, the painter called down. "Can I help?" he asked.

Again, Gemarakup barely favored him with a glance. "No thanks," he said. "This is really tough stuff."

With that, he and his friend disappeared, away from smelly painting and little sisters who ate too loudly.

It wasn't until two nights later, at the Finkels' resplendent *Shabbos* table, that Gemarakup finally got the *sugya* explained to him. Though he posed his questions to his father, it was their *Shabbos* guest, Yossie Fein, who finally helped him understand the *Gemara's p'shat*. Which wasn't surprising, really: throughout the meal Yossie, a young man in his early twenties who was learning in a nearby *yeshivah*, had proved himself to be a fascinating and understandable educator, as well as a *talmid*

chacham. He held Tamar spellbound with his recital of *midrashim* on the *parashah*, and was even able to hold his own in a Talmudic argument with Mr. Finkel.

After dinner, Yossie had insisted on helping to clear the table. While Yossie was busy stacking plates and cups carefully in the kitchen sink, Gemarakup turned to his father, who was still sitting in his place at the table.

"That's some great guy, that Yossie," Gemarakup remarked. "How long has he been in the neighborhood?"

"Oh, quite a while," his father answered.

"So why in the world didn't he ever come to us before? He's terrific," Gemarakup looked eagerly at his father. "Do you think he would learn with me after *benching*?"

Tamar, who was (again!) crunching a bright red apple, turned a quizzical eye on her older brother. "You don't want Yossie to learn with you," she declared, as she made her way to the front hallway. "You want to learn with this!"

Tamar whisked a black hat out from behind her and plopped it squarely down on Gemarakup's puzzled head!

Can you guess what Tamar means — and why Gemarakup would want to learn with a hat? For the solution, turn to page 79.

VI.
Of Cabbages and Rings

One of Gemarakup's most irritating habits, Mrs. Finkel used to say, was the way he had of disappearing between the pages of a book, not to return to the real world until the last word had been read and the covers thumped closed. When the book was a good one, nothing could break through his trance. Nothing, that is, except . . .

"Cookies! I smell chocolate-chip cookies!" Gemarakup said half to himself. He threw the latest book he'd gotten out of the school library, a short history of the Jews of Syria, down on his desk and raced down the stairs in hot pursuit of the irresistible smell of baking dough.

When he reached the kitchen, he found his mother just pulling out a tray from the oven. A quick glance showed that these were no run-of-the-mill chocolate-chip cookies, however; the cookies that were coming out looked crisp, were golden in color, and were oddly shaped.

But they smelled delicious and Gemarakup, ever courageous when it came to trying out new goodies, immediately asked for one.

"Mmm . . . they're great," Gemarakup assured his mother, as he munched the crispy treat. "But wait a minute. What's this?" he asked, wrinkling his nose. "Imma, you dropped something into your dough!"

Gingerly, he pulled out a small slip of paper that had somehow gotten baked into the cookie.

His mother, far from looking chagrined, smiled broadly. "Read it, Yisrael David," she said.

Gemarakup carefully uncrumpled the small paper. "Your search will be rewarded," he read. He looked at his laughing mother, puzzled. "What in the world does it mean?"

"That wasn't just a cookie you ate, Yisrael David," his mother answered. "That was a Chinese fortune cookie!"

Gemarakup answered his mother's smile with one of his own. "Like they give out in Chinese restaurants?"

"That's right. You bake a little saying right into the cookie and serve it for dessert with Chinese tea. Before I started baking the cookies, I wrote out a whole bunch of those little papers. It's a lot of fun eating the cookies and reading the fortunes inside."

That little culinary mystery solved, Gemarakup prepared to test his fortune again with another cookie. But his mother, used to such incursions, quickly headed him off by grabbing the tray.

"Oh, no. They're not really for us, and I've got to have some left. Which I won't, if I let you start eating all of them up."

"Who are you baking them for, Imma?" Gemarakup asked.

"The *yeshivah* dinner," his mother explained. "We're having 'International Night' as a fundraiser. I'm doing Chinese desserts. Slugger's mother is making chicken teriyaki — that's Japanese. We'll have souffles from France, pasta salad from Italy, even falafel from *Eretz Yisrael!*"

"Sounds great," Gemarakup said, his mouth watering and his hand automatically hovering over the next batch of cookies which his mother pulled out of the oven. "Is anyone making anything that's just plain Jewish, though?" he asked, hastily removing his fingers as his mother only half-jokingly brandished her spatula to defend her cookies.

"Sure," Mrs. Finkel answered. "Mrs. Feinerman is making gefilte fish, and Mrs. Navon is making stuffed cabbage. As a matter of fact, I promised to give her my recipe. I'll call her as soon as I finish here."

"Well, I hope you make a lot of money for the school," Gemarakup said. "And now, if this tasting session is over . . ." he added, with a hopeful glance at the cookies.

"It sure is," his mother said, trying to sound stern.

Accepting the inevitable, Gemarakup went back to his room, to forget about Chinese cookies and travel back to the Syria of two centuries ago.

Suddenly, the sound of his mother's anguished shout shot forth from the kitchen.

"My ring! Who's seen my ring?" she cried.

Gemarakup, sensing the unusual hysteria in her voice, took the steps two at a time. "What ring?" he asked, looking anxiously at his mother's flushed face.

"My . . . my wedding ring! It's gone!"

"Gone?"

Mrs. Finkel took a deep breath, obviously trying to calm down. In a quieter tone of voice, she continued. "I was kneading the dough for the cookies and I didn't want my ring to get dirty so I took it off and put it on the shelf over the sink. And now, it's gone. My wedding ring! From my *chasunah*!"

To his horror, Gemarakup saw his mother's eyes grow moist. Imma *never* cried over something lost or broken! This wedding ring must really mean something special to her.

"Don't worry, Imma," he said, trying to sound as reassuring as he could. "We'll find it."

But here Gemarakup was wrong. Though they cleaned up that kitchen in a way that reminded him of Pesach, though they combed every inch and then some, there was no sign of the ring.

After more than an hour of fruitless searching, Mrs. Finkel finally gave up. She had calmed down somewhat, nevertheless she seemed subdued. "Thanks, kids," she told Gemarakup and Tamar, who had joined them. Then she sighed. "I guess it must have gone down the drain, or just plain disappeared into thin air. Anyway, we can't go on doing this all night. You kids get into pajamas and go to bed, or you won't be able to wake up tomorrow."

Although he listened to his mother's admonitions to get into bed, sleep did not come easily to Gemarakup. He kept thinking about his mother, remembering how beautiful she looked in her wedding album, and how upset she'd been over losing her wedding ring. His father was working late. What would he say when he came home and found out? He wouldn't be angry — but would he also be upset?

Gemarakup's eyes finally closed. He could hear his mother downstairs giving Mrs. Navon the recipe for her famous cabbage and telling her what had happened to her ring. Words drifted through his sleepy mind . . . ring . . . missing . . . cabbage . . . cookies . . .

Suddenly, Gemarakup leaped out of bed. Taking the steps three at a time (and almost breaking his neck when he missed one!) he found himself in the kitchen in a few seconds.

"Imma, quick! Get me the cookies!"

Is Gemarakup suffering an acute attack of the munchies? Or is there another reason he wants the cookies? For the answer, turn to page 82.

VII.
The New Kid in Town

"et Freedom Ring." The words of the traditional patriotic American song took on a new meaning, Gemarakup mused, if one was a sixth-grader trapped in a particularly boring social studies class. Let it ring . . . Oh please, let it ring . . .

Brrrring! The school bell finally gave its shrill cry. Recess! Freedom! Thirty-one boys gave a shout, clambered out of seats, jumped into raincoats, and flew out the door.

Only one stayed behind.

Gemarakup watched the ball approach swiftly through the slate gray sky. His muscles tensed; he swung. Crack! With a satisfying smack bat met ball, sending it flying back where it had come from. Gemarakup dropped the bat and ran towards first base, his feet dragging in the thick, muddy ooze that was the *yeshivah* ballfield. He reached first base, sending a shower of wet earth all around him.

Slugger, up after Gemarakup, once again earned his nickname, batting a double. Chezky Schwartz struck out, much to his teammates' chagrin, but then Yossie Brown came through with a single, sending a triumphant and filthy Gemarakup sliding into home plate just before the bell announced the end of recess.

"What's the score?" Gemarakup asked, as he and his classmates turned towards the school building.

"Seventeen — Fourteen, ours," Slugger answered, wiping a muddy cheek with an equally muddy hand. "And three innings to go!"

Gemarakup grinned. "Maybe we should call the Guiness Book of World Records. How long has this game been going on, anyway?"

Slugger answered his friend's smile with one of his own. "We started, let's see, it was Sunday. And today's Thursday. Not bad."

Indeed, the softball game that was being played between the two sixth-grade teams was making sports history in Yeshivah Ahavas Chesed. The boys couldn't say if it was the chilly, wet weather that kept them exercising to keep warm, or if it was just a fluke, but this game was breaking records for runs batted in. And it certainly seemed that it would last forever. Five days of recess play for six innings — not bad, as Slugger said. At this rate they could expect this game to go on through next week — and the rematch to continue through next month!

The boys slid noisily into their seats and opened their math books. As he pondered the mysteries of square roots, Gemarakup's gaze wandered over the classroom. His eyes fell on a smallish student sitting hunched over his book a few rows away. The one student in the sixth grade who had not joined in the game.

Sasha.

Gemarakup's conscience suddenly gave him a painful stab. He'd completely forgotten . . .

Sasha Ushkin was a new kid. New to the class, new to the country. Though, not, as were many of his Russian counterparts, new to *Yiddishkeit*: Sasha's father was one of the best known *ba'alei teshuvah* in the city of Kiev, and had found his way to a Torah way of life during the difficult days of the Soviet regime. When hundreds of thousands of other Soviet Jews were finally allowed to leave, Sasha's father had actually stayed on until he was certain that his students in Kiev would have someone to teach them in his stead. Sasha spoke English well, and with only a little tutoring would soon be able to keep up with his sixth-grade American class.

But though it seemed that Sasha's road would not be as difficult as many other former Soviets had to travel, still, life wasn't easy when you were new to a culture, a school, a class. And so Rabbi Eliach had prevailed upon the sixth-graders to be nice, to be friendly — in short, to make Sasha feel at home and help him adjust.

And what had Gemarakup done? Played softball.

But I tried, Gemarakup told his conscience. I asked him to join us in the yard during recess three times this week. Every time, he said no.

And so what did you do then, his conscience asked remorselessly.

Umm . . . nothing.

Did you try to find out why he didn't want to come out and play?

No.

Did you offer to teach him softball?

No.

Did you do your best?

Absolutely not.

Are you going to do better?

You betcha!

Gemarakup and Sasha walked together towards the Finkel home. Gemarakup, having listened to the promptings of his conscience, had wasted no time in inviting the new boy to come home with him after school. Sasha, he found, was a fun kid who was very open and easy to talk with. Though he liked his new home, the Russian boy confided to his new-found friend, his dream was to move to *Eretz Yisrael*.

The two were avidly discussing the pros and cons of living in Israel when they finally reached Gemarakup's house.

Mrs. Finkel met them at the door. She took one look at her son and gave a loud sigh. "Those sneakers aren't coming onto my clean carpets," she announced. "Leave them on the doorstep, Yisrael David. And then go upstairs and out of those filthy clothes. That is, if you can find anything to wear in that disaster area you call your closet." Shaking her head ruefully, she continued. "That's the fourth pair of pants you've gone through in as many days. Are you a student or a garbage man, Yisrael David?"

Her son smiled. "Just a baseball hero, Imma, playing in a very wet field. It's not my fault it's been raining all week," he said.

"Another reason to move to *Eretz Yisrael*," Sasha interjected. "It only rains four months a year. Hardly any mud at all. Look how much more baseball you could play."

"Yeah. Maybe I'll be like Choni HaMa'agal. Only I won't stand in a circle — I'll stand on a pitcher's mound."

The two of them laughed. Mrs. Finkel looked curiously at the unfamiliar face.

"Who's your friend, Yisrael David?" she asked.

Gemarakup made the introductions. After he changed his clothes, he and Sasha went to the kitchen to enjoy a snack before homework.

The hours passed quickly. The boys learned, played computer games, and looked at Gemarakup's *gedolim* collection. Too soon, it was time for Sasha to go home.

Gemarakup walked him part of the way. The weather continued to be nasty, with a light drizzle that misted up Gemarakup's glasses and sent shivers down his back, but the rain couldn't dampen his cheerfulness. Sasha wasn't a *chesed* case — he was a good guy! A new friend!

"Listen, Sash, tomorrow you come with me during recess and I'll get you a place on the team," Gemarakup said, eager to make Sasha feel like one of the gang.

Suddenly, the atmosphere grew chillier than the biting wind outside. "I'd rather not," Sasha said.

Gemarakup, taken aback, fell silent. Then, brightening, he spoke. "Sasha, if you don't know how to play softball, I'll teach you."

"I know how to play," his companion said shortly. "I just . . . can't."

"Well, how about just coming to watch," Gemarakup persisted. "You know, the whole class is into this game. If you want to be part of the class, it would be a good idea to join us."

"I can't," Sasha declared firmly. He looked up at the threatening sky. "It's going to start to pour," he said, "you'd better get home."

With a sigh and a wave, Gemarakup turned away. He walked slowly, despite the rising wind. He couldn't make this kid out. He seemed to want to belong, he was a good guy — but why this weird refusal to take part in something so important to the class?

As he made his way through the thickening fog, a moving van rattled past through a large puddle, sending a spray of dirty water all over Gemarakup's legs. "Oh no, Imma's going to kill me!" he groaned. "That's the fifth pair of pants this week!"

Gemarakup stopped short. "Wait a minute. It could be . . . it *has* to be!"

Gemarakup turned and raced after his new classmate's retreating figure. "Sash, wait up!" he called.

"What is it?" Sasha asked his panting friend, concerned.

Gemarakup grabbed him by the arm. "Come to my house, Sasha, just for a minute. It's raining too hard to talk out here. And we've got something to talk about."

Can you guess what Gemarakup is going to say? For the solution, turn to page 84.

VIII.
Gemarakup and the Great Purim Caper

he young man stared grimly into his small hand mirror. One tough kid stared back: heavy brows sticking up out of dark glasses; dark, fuzzy mustache and the shadowy trace of a beard; a horrendous and angry scar giving a sinister cast to the pale, bloodless cheeks.

With a little movement of aversion, the young tough turned away from the mirror to the white-clad, red-cheeked bride standing next to him. Finally, gruffly, he spoke.

"So what do you think, Tamar?"

Tamar gave a final pat to the veil that kept falling into her eyes. "Well, Gemarakup, if you wanted to look horrible, you've done a great job, I'll tell you that."

Gemarakup laughed, then winced. That stupid mustache had been glued on, and any sudden facial movement really hurt!

"Horrible's the word, this Purim!" he said gaily.

"And speaking of horrible, that must be Slugger downstairs," Tamar giggled, as she heard the doorbell give a clangorous ring.

Gemarakup dared not smile again. Instead, he raced down the steps, two at a time, to open the door.

There before him stood another young hoodlum, this one sporting a handlebar mustache and a skull on his black leather jacket. His skin was a suspicious shade of green.

"Ready, Gemarakup?" Slugger asked, trying to deepen his voice.

"Just a sec. I want to say goodbye to my mom."

"Well hurry up," Slugger said impatiently. "The guys are waiting for us at the corner."

Gemarakup jammed his hands into the pockets of his leather jacket, hunched his shoulders, and ambled into the kitchen, where his mother was putting the finishing touches on the *shalach manos* baskets that would be delivered within the next few hours. She looked up at her son's entrance.

"Are you going to your *rebbe's* now?" she asked.

"Yup. Slugger 'n me are meeting the guys down on 45th Street. We thought it'd be nice for us to all go together."

His mother put a bag of freshly baked hamantaschen into a lovely wicker basket she was preparing for an elderly neighbor. "Have fun, Yisrael David, but make sure you get back by eleven. We've got a lot of delivering to do before the *seudah*. Oh, and on the way back, stop at Uncle Ezra's and give him back his *siddur*. I borrowed it this morning in *shul* and forgot to return it." Gemarakup carelessly placed the small leather-bound volume into his pocket, waved a black gloved hand, and walked out.

He felt oddly disappointed. His mother hadn't even mentioned his costume! Not that he could blame her, really. He knew that his parents didn't particularly like the idea of him and his friends dressing up as a bunch of motorcycle bums. Imma had been so excited about his original idea. He had planned on dressing up as the *Rambam*, fez and all. But all the other guys wanted to dress up like a street gang, and Gemarakup didn't feel like being left out. His father hadn't exactly forbidden him from joining them, but Abba had made it pretty clear that he would prefer a son who looked like a *gadol* to one who looked like an escaped convict.

For once, though, Gemarakup hadn't listened. And now here he was, self-consciously walking the streets in jeans and a black jacket.

He felt a little less conspicuous when he joined the rest of his *chevrah*, each sporting his own leather jacket.

There was a lot of raucous laughter as the boys set off for their *rebbe's* house. Slugger made "va-room" sounds as he revved up a non-existent engine. With a whoop and a shout, the motorcycle gang of Yeshivah Ahavas Chesed was off!

It should have been fun. It sounded like fun, what with the shrill laughter, loud cheering, and Slugger's endless va-rooms. It looked like fun, this convivial and joking bunch of friends joshing each other with Purim Torah. So why, thought Gemarakup as he walked next to Slugger, wasn't it fun at all?

Perhaps it was the look that an elderly lady had given them as they'd passed her on the street that cast a pall on Gemarakup's merriment. There'd been trouble last month with a gang of toughs who'd vandalized an old age home and frightened its elderly occupants; maybe the lady was remembering the incident as she walked pass Gemarakup and his friends. The thought made Gemarakup uncomfortable.

And then there was his friends' increasingly wild behavior. Gemarakup began to suspect that his *rebbes* were right in insisting that *yeshivah* boys always dress properly. Dressed like thugs, his friends were beginning to act like thugs: loud, pushy, a little uncouth.

But it was Purim, and he was going to have fun. No matter what!

The pushing, shoving crowd of boys turned the corner towards Rabbi Eliach's house. Suddenly, their loud laughter was drowned out by the piercing wail of a siren. A white Ford van with a flashing red light on its roof passed by. Then, with a teeth-grinding screech of its brakes, the van swerved and came to a halt, right in front of the boys.

A stocky man wearing a black turtleneck, jeans, and a low-slung cap jumped out of the car, leaving two blue-uni-formed men behind in the back seat. The black-clad man pulled out a small leather card case and flipped it open. "Detective O'Rourke, Fourteenth Precinct, Plainclothes Division," he snarled. "Let's see your I.D.s."

The boys gaped, speechless. The police? I.D.s? Help!

"We . . . we don't have any identification, Officer," Yossie Brown yelped. "We were . . . we were just . . ." He came to a lame halt. How in the world could he explain Purim to this angry cop?

Anyway, it didn't look like the policeman was going to give them a chance to explain anything. The plainclothesman gave a brusque nod to his colleagues, and the two uniformed policemen jumped out of the van.

Slugger made another attempt at explanation. "Sir, it's Purim, see . . ."

O'Rourke gave him a withering glance. "Quiet, punk," he snarled. "We've had enough trouble with you gangs this month. Never heard of no Purim, and I'm not interested." He turned to the uniformed cops. "Frisk 'em, and get ready to run 'em in," he ordered tersely.

Gemarakup watched in mounting horror as the two policemen searched the boys — none too gently — for knives and guns.

The policemen had already confiscated four cap guns, assorted ammunition (none of it live!), and several hamantaschen, when they finally approached Gemarakup. One of the cops pulled him over by his jacket collar and began to search him. The other put his hand into Gemarakup's pocket. Out came the *siddur*.

"Hey, lookit this, the punk can read," the policeman shouted. He gently placed the *siddur* into Officer O'Rourke's hand.

Gemarakup, pale and shaken, watched as O'Rourke opened the *siddur*. The policeman flipped through the first page or two, but the words of *Modeh Ani* seemed meaningless to him, and he turned away and carefully placed the *siddur* in his van.

Gemarakup sighed. Now more than ever, he wished he'd dressed up as the *Rambam*. A *gadol b'Torah* and a genius — there was a man who would know how to deal with this problem!

Gemarakup's eyes narrowed; his pale cheeks flushed. Wait a minute! The *Rambam*! The *siddur* . . . It had to be!

O'Rourke turned to the policemen. "Get 'em into the back of the van. We're running them in — on suspicion of vandalism, loitering, and intent to commit damage."

Gemarakup, his hands on his hips, strode towards O'Rourke. He looked O'Rourke straight in the eye. "Nobody starts up with my gang," Gemarakup declared in a dangerous growl. "You wanna take us in — you're gonna have to fight us first."

Has Gemarakup gone nuts? Or does he know something we don't know? For the solution, turn to page 87.

IX.
The Rebbe's Mystery

emarakup's eyes were riveted to the sight: a one-armed man hanging upon the gallows, his face a blank.

Slowly, furtively, Gemarakup lifted his head and peered in front of him. He sighed with relief. No, he wasn't being watched. He was safe for now.

He thought for a moment, then picked up a pencil and carefully wrote down the letter D. He watched with bated breath to see what the response would be.

After a moment he gave a sigh of relief. The choice was correct; the letter D existed in the secret message. The man on the gallows remained incomplete, at least for now.

And so the game of Hangman continued its course.

The tournament between Slugger and Gemarakup had begun earlier that morning, during a particularly dull class on *dikduk*. Slugger had scribbled a tic-tac-toe board on the back of a notebook and passed it on to his friend. Though Gemarakup was usually a diligent student, there was just so much grammar a kid could take, and he had carefully sent it back, his "X" marked in the corner. From tic-tac-toe they'd gone on to Dots, Jotto, and now, Hangman.

It was one way of passing the time peacefully.

At least, until Rabbi Eliach showed up behind them, fingering his beard and staring at Slugger's unfinished message.

"If you put in a "K" and a "Y" you'll see what Nachman Moshe has to say," Rabbi Eliach said quietly.

Almost hypnotized with embarrassment, Gemarakup wrote in the letters and read the secret message his friend had come up with: I hate *dikduk*, don't you?

Scarlet-faced, both boys looked down at their desks, their notebooks, their feet: anywhere but at their *rebbe,* whose disappointed gaze hurt more than any slap.

"So you hate *dikduk,* Nachman Moshe?" Rabbi Eliach said, still in that quiet, unrelenting voice. "And is that an excuse for such behavior?"

"We're sorry, *Rebbe,* really we are," Gemarakup said in a small voice. "We didn't mean any *chutzpah* or anything, really. It's just so . . . so . . . well, it's so boring!"

"Yisrael David, nothing is boring if you concentrate on learning it correctly," Rabbi Eliach said. "And nothing is interesting if you won't use your brains on it." The *rebbe's* eyes glinted from behind his thick glasses, and a small smile played upon his lips. "I'll tell you what, Yisrael David. Your specialty is solving mysteries through stories, right?"

Gemarakup, thoroughly perplexed, nodded his head.

"Sometime today, in one of my *shiurim,* I am going to solve a mystery myself by using a story. I challenge you to listen carefully all morning — and see if you can tell me what it was!"

Gemarakup smiled in relief and delight. Not only was his *rebbe* not going to punish him for his behavior — but he was going to have the chance to solve a mystery as well!

The rest of the morning flew by, as Gemarakup, model student, his brow furrowed and brain working in high gear, listened and participated and concentrated. He discovered several surprising things: that his *rebbe,* as usual, had been right, and that if a student thought about what he was learning then the stuff became much more interesting; that even *dikduk* could be, if not incredibly fascinating, then at least palatable; and that time could move very swiftly if one was working hard. The only thing he could not discover, though, was the mystery that his *rebbe* had talked about. Through the lesson in *Chumash* on the sin of the Golden Calf, through a complicated *Mishnah* on the *halachos* of an *eiruv* on *Shabbos,* and through a long *shiur* in *Gemara* that discussed Queen Esther and Sarah *Imeinu* he listened, and thought, and listened some more.

As the morning drew to an end, Gemarakup was ready to admit it: he was stumped. Once more, he carefully reviewed in his mind all the things he had learned.

Suddenly, he jumped up in his seat. "I've got it, *Rebbe,* " he cried.

Rabbi Eliach laughed. "Hold on, Yisrael David," he said. "Got what?"

"The answer! The mystery that you talked about! You just followed the lesson of Rabbi Akiva!"

Can you guess what Rabbi Eliach and Rabbi Akiva have in common? For the answer, turn to page 89.

X.
The Graffiti Getaway

r. Finkel looked impatiently at his gold wristwatch. "Seven-thirty. He's already half an hour late," he said.

Gemarakup laughed. "Half an hour's not late. Not for Uncle Ezra."

Mr. Finkel, to whom promptness was a much sought after virtue, gave a deep sigh. He glanced ruefully at the luminous dial. "Your Uncle Ezra is a great man, Yisrael David, but when it comes to going with him anywhere . . . you need the patience of Hillel."

"Eliezer." The word came out sharply from Mrs. Finkel's mouth, not so much a rebuke as a warning. Caution: *lashon hara* up ahead!

Mr. Finkel acknowledged her wisdom and grew silent. Moments later, a loud honk was followed by a sharp knock — and that was followed by the cheerful grin of Gemarakup's Uncle Ezra.

"Hi, gang! Ready for pizza?" He gave a contrite glance at Mr. Finkel. "Sorry I'm so late, Eli. I had some arrangements to make that took longer than I expected. But wait'll you hear what they are."

"What's up, Uncle Ezra?" Gemarakup asked curiously. "What kind of arrangements?"

"You know that little *shul* up on Robert Street?" Uncle Ezra began.

"Robert Street? Where's that?"

"You wouldn't know the neighborhood, Yisrael David," Mr. Finkel explained. "It used to have a large Jewish population, but some years ago it changed. Became very tough, a high crime area. Most of the Jews moved away."

"That's right," Ezra took up the story. "And only a few elderly people remained. *Shul* after *shul* closed down too, and finally only one, *Aishel Avraham,* was left. They get a *minyan*, just barely, during the week. On *Shabbos* they may have up to twenty people *davening*."

"But what does this have to do with you?" Tamar asked impatiently. This was all very interesting, but she was hungry! Uncle Ezra had promised them all a pizza dinner at a new restaurant, and Tamar was finding it hard to wait.

"I'll tell you what it has to do with me. I just found out that *Aishel Avraham* has a large *genizah* in its basement."

"What's a *genizah*?" Tamar asked, curious despite herself.

"A place where old or ripped *sefarim* are kept," her father explained.

"These old *genizahs* are almost always full of rare old books," Uncle Ezra finished happily. "That's how I've gotten many of my most precious *sefarim*. I'm sure I'll add a few to my collection."

Gemarakup's eyes lit up. His uncle loved his collection of old and rare *sefarim*. How Uncle Ezra would enjoy adding to it!

"There's only one problem," Ezra said. "I've been given permission to take what I want, but only if I take everything with me and dispose of the entire *genizah* properly, even those things that are unusable. There are eight or nine large boxes, they told me — more than will fit into my little car."

Mr. Finkel grinned. "And so you want me to do some chauffeuring for you in the van?"

"You got it."

Minutes later they entered the gleaming vehicle: Mr. Finkel, still pleased with the new minivan that he'd bought the week before; Mrs. Finkel, glancing at her watch; an excited Gemarakup and his even more excited Uncle Ezra; and a plaintive and hungry Tamar (would they *ever* get to the restaurant?). They sped through the dark streets, through neighborhoods that grew increasingly run-down. Finally, they reached a squat two-story building surrounded by a rocky, overgrown garden encircled by barbed wire. Gemarakup gave a shiver: this was sure a lot different from his own warm, welcoming *shul*!

Tamar had fallen asleep in the back seat of the van. Mr. Finkel looked out the window at the blighted scene before him. "I don't want to leave Tamar and Imma here alone," he said.

"No problem, Eli," Uncle Ezra said. "Me and my nephew here can take care of all the *shlepping*. Right, Gemarakup?"

"Sure, Uncle Ezra. You can stay here in the car, Abba."

"Mr. Flohr, that's the *gabbai*, was going to meet me here. And here he is," Uncle Ezra pointed to an elderly man hobbling up the street.

"Please try to make it quick, Ezra, the kids have school tomorrow," Mr. Finkel said, as Gemarakup and his uncle hopped out of the van.

Mr. Flohr was a grizzled old man with an unexpectedly charming and youthful smile. He shook hands with Uncle Ezra and Gemarakup, then shakily pulled out an enormous ring of keys.

"We've been having some flooding in the basement," Mr. Flohr explained, as he pulled open the steel door. "And I'm afraid if we don't get rid of the *sefarim* soon, they'll all rot."

Finally, they were inside the darkness of the *shul*. Their

footsteps echoed eerily on the uncarpeted wooden floors; the dim light of a lone *yahrzeit* lamp cast frightening shadows. It was quiet inside, with a stillness that sent shivers up Gemarakup's spine.

Finally, Mr. Flohr reached a panel and switched on the electricity. Harsh fluorescent light flooded the lobby. The sinister atmosphere disappeared. Gemarakup saw before him a fairly shabby room lined with memorial plaques.

Mr. Flohr silently pointed to a set of steps leading to the basement. The three gingerly walked down the rickety staircase. Mr. Flohr came to another light switch and flipped it on.

Gemarakup didn't know exactly what he had expected to see — An old unpainted room, perhaps, full of chipped chairs and rotting benches, or boxes and boxes of yellowed *sefarim*. He certainly didn't expect to see the sight that met his astonished eyes: a young man, about sixteen-years-old, in jeans and T-shirt, carefully writing "Jews Get Out" in garish red spray paint.

As shocked as Gemarakup was, it didn't compare to the dismay that the surprised intruder obviously felt. With a muttered oath he spun around, brutally pushed Mr. Flohr to the side, and ran up the stairs two at a time.

Before the three had a chance to react, the room was plunged into blackness.

"I'm going after him," Uncle Ezra said urgently, in a voice that sounded strange to Gemarakup. "You stay here, Gemarakup — make sure that Mr. Flohr is okay. And see if you can get the lights on."

Though Gemarakup would have liked nothing better than to join in the chase, he realized that it wouldn't be fair to leave the old, shaken man by himself. He gave Mr. Flohr a chance to catch his breath, then slowly, ever so slowly, led him up the stairs in the darkness.

"What happened to the lights?" Gemarakup said half to himself.

"There's a switch right near the main door," Mr. Flohr explained, breathing heavily. "If that . . . that hoodlum pulled it, it cuts off all the electricity."

The two reached the top just as the lights went back on. In the lobby, Gemarakup saw his father, Uncle Ezra, and two uniformed policemen.

No sign of the fugitive however.

"I don't understand where he could have gone," Uncle Ezra said, shaking his head in puzzlement. "I was only a few minutes behind him."

"Did he escape the same way he got in?" Gemarakup asked.

"Doesn't look that way," his father answered him. "These policemen were passing by, and I called them in as soon as Ezra told me what was happening. It seems there's a broken window right near the front door. We didn't notice it in the dark, but it's clear that the hoodlum entered through there."

"So why are you so sure he didn't go out the same way he came in?" Gemarakup asked, intrigued by the problem.

"I was parked in front of the *shul* the entire time, and I am absolutely certain no one came out — no one, that is, except for Ezra."

"Well, if he didn't go out that way, how about through the garden?"

"Not possible," one of the policemen said shortly. "If he'd gone into the garden, he'd be trapped there. The only way out of the garden is through the synagogue entrance itself."

"That's right," Mr. Flohr added. "We had some trouble with these tough kids, who were making the garden a hangout, so we surrounded it with barbed wire. If he went into the garden, he could only get out by coming back in here and going out the front entrance. But are you sure he's not hiding there?" the old man said anxiously, shivering.

"He's not in the garden," Ezra reassured him. "The officers here used their flashlights to check. Not a soul there."

Mr. Finkel looked puzzled. "He's not in the basement, he's not in the garden, and he didn't leave the *shul* — where can he be?"

"Are you certain he's not in the *beis medrash* itself?" Gemarakup asked.

"We searched while you were downstairs, Gemarakup," Ezra answered, "but there's no sign of him. Still, you're welcome to look."

Gemarakup followed Mr. Flohr into the main *beis medrash*. He saw several tables surrounded by chipped wooden benches, an unimposing *aron kodesh* covered with a frayed blue velvet curtain, a few *shtenders*. Memorial plaques hung on the whitewashed walls. Gemarakup's eyes roamed upwards to the cobweb-covered chandelier that hung from the ceiling, not far from a dust-encrusted skylight.

"No sign of him here," Mr. Flohr announced. "He's not in the *shul*."

"And he's not in the garden," one of the policemen added.

"And he didn't leave by the front door," Mr. Finkel sighed.

Uncle Ezra looked at his nephew. "Well, Gemarakup, we're all stumped. You solve the mystery — where in the world did the hoodlum disappear to?"

Gemarakup didn't reply. He was lost in thought. Something he'd said tonight . . . something he'd seen tonight . . . something should give him a clue . . . something — Of course!

"I know where that thug is!" Gemarakup shouted. "Let's get to the garden — quick!"

Can you figure out where the hoodlum is hiding? Turn to page 90 for the solution.

XI.
Gemarakup Cracks the Code

2-5-200-0-700-60-300-0-3-1-50-200-0-6-
9-7-300-90-5-0-200-8-9-100-0-60-300-
200   — Shuey

emarakup stared at the numbers written neatly on an otherwise blank sheet of paper. The numbers stared back.

Pinchas Epstein, who had handed the mysterious paper to Gemarakup just moments earlier, looked hopefully at his friend. "Well?" he asked.

"Well, what?" Gemarakup shot back, completely bewildered.

"What do you mean, what? What does it mean?"

Gemarakup sighed. Pinchas was a good bunkmate and a close "camp friend," but he was not always easy to understand. Particularly when he chose to talk in riddles.

"What does it mean?" Gemarakup repeated. "It means that you have given me a paper full of numbers. Now, Pin," he continued with just a touch of impatience in his voice, "in words of one syllable would you kindly tell me what you're talking about."

Pinchas grinned. "Look, you're the big-shot detective. And I've got a case for you."

Gemarakup's eyes lit up. Here in camp, chances for solving mysteries were few and far between. "Okay. Shoot."

"I got this letter today at mail call," Pinchas explained. "It's from . . ."

"Let me guess. From someone called Shuey."

Pinchas gave Gemarakup a look of wonder. "How'd you know that?"

Gemarakup rolled his eyes. "From the only word on the whole page. See," he pointed to the paper, "Shuey."

"Oh. Well, Shuey is a friend of mine from school. Goes to Camp Shalom. Good kid, super-bright."

Gemarakup was conscious of an overwhelming urge to yawn. "Spare me the details of your schoolmates, Pin. Get to the point of the letter."

"Yeah. Well, Shuey loves puzzles, riddles, things like that. He enjoys stumping me, asking me things like how is an eraser like a burst balloon and waiting for me to say I haven't the slightest idea. I wrote to him last week, and complained that he owed me a letter. And this," Pinchas ended ruefully, "is his answer. Only, it makes no sense."

Pinchas looked once more at the paper and handed it back to Gemarakup. "I know what he wants me to do. He wants me to write to him, asking him what he meant. But I'll beat him — that is, we'll beat him."

Gemarakup's eyes sparkled. "I get it. You want me to crack the code."

"That's it! Would you help?"

Pinchas got no reply. Gemarakup was already concentrating, peering closely at each of the mysterious digits. He grabbed a pencil from a nearby shelf and scribbled a few lines, muttering to himself as he worked.

"Got it!" came a crow of triumph. "He writes: BET YOU CAN'T FIGURE THIS OUT."

Pinchas cast another amazed look at his friend. He had heard of his prowess as a detective, but he had never seen him in action before!

"How'd you figure it out?" he asked admiringly.

"This code is very simple. It's just *gematria*, transformed to English letters," Gemarakup explained.

"I realized right away that the numbers must each stand for a letter. I tried the simplest method to see if it would work: 'A' is one, 'B' is two, and so on. Usually, the eleventh letter of the alphabet, 'K', becomes eleven, but when I saw the large three-digit numbers I realized that wouldn't work. So I used the same method that we use in *gematria*: after 'J,' which is ten, comes 'K,' twenty; 'L,' thirty; and so on. This way, 'S' becomes one hundred, and 'T,' which follows, is two hundred.

"That took care of almost everything. The only question, then, was the number zero, which came up very often. I guessed that zero meant that the word was ended and a new word was starting. I just made a chart of each number's letter, substituted it in the code, and came up with Shuey's message. No problem!"

Pinchas's face lit up with a delighted grin. "I can't wait to write to Shuey and tell him we cracked his code!" he said.

Gemarakup's face took on a mischievous look. "No, don't just write him. Wait a minute." Once again, he scribbled figures furiously on the paper. Finally, he looked up. "Send him this message, with my best regards," he said.

TREV NV Z SZIW LMV

Pinchas's large blue eyes traveled from the note to Gemarakup's face and back again. "Huh?"

"It's a code, Pin," Gemarakup explained.

"I figured that much out," his friend answered. "But what does it say?"

"Like *gematria*, it's a method *Chazal* sometimes use to understand certain words in *Tanach*," Gemarakup explained. "In Hebrew, the code is called '*At-bash*,' which stands for '*aleph-taf, beis-shin*.'

"You see," he continued, "you write out the first part of the alphabet, like this:

A B C D E F G H I J K L M

"Underneath, you continue the alphabet, but you start at the right side, like this:

A B C D E F G H I J K L M
Z Y X W V U T S R Q P O N

"Then you simply substitute, 'Z' for 'A,' 'Y' for 'B,' and so on. In Hebrew we do *aleph* for *tuf*, *beis* for *shin*, which is why it's called '*at-bash*.'

"If you substitute, you'll find that I've simply made a polite request to Shuey: 'Give me a hard one.' "

Pinchas laughed. "That he'll do, I'm sure."

Gemarakup was a devoted regular of Camp Kayitz's "early bird *shiurim*". Twice a week, boys who wanted to do so rose in the misty pre-dawn hours, *davened netz*, and then learned while the rest of the camp soundly slept. The trilling of birds, the cool, moist air, the smell of the cocoa that awaited the young *talmidei chachamim* at the end of *shiur*, and, of course, the serious learning that one could do in the quiet hours of morning, all made these "early bird" hours an unforgettable highlight of the summer.

Which made Pinchas's antics that morning so much more annoying.

All through the *shiur* Pinchas hissed, threw meaningful looks, and made faces at Gemarakup. While the others were discussing the *halachos* of *Shabbos* as learned from the *Gemara*, Pinchas was throwing spitballs. Getting Gemarakup's attention was more important, it seemed, than anything the *rebbe* had to say.

Finally, with *shiur* over, Pinchas could have his say.

"What is it?" Gemarakup asked wearily.

"Your code must have really blown Shuey's mind," Pinchas said excitedly. "My counselor picked up our mail yesterday and he forgot to give me my letter until this morning. The envelope was postmarked from Shuey. But when I opened it, I found . . . this!"

Pinchas held a paper aloft with a flourish. "It's completely blank. I'll bet Shuey was so frazzled by your 'at-bash' code, he made a mistake and forgot to put his letter in the envelope." Pinchas laughed heartily at his friend's error.

Gemarakup, though, did not laugh. Instead, he reached for the paper. "Give me that a minute," he said thoughtfully.

After a moment he looked up. "Your friend Shuey wasn't frazzled at all. He knew exactly what he was doing when he sent this paper!

"You know, Pinchas, if you didn't spend so much time sending spitballs, and listened to *shiur* instead, you might be able to crack some codes without my help. Now let's go get a cup of cocoa — and make a stop at the oven. We need the cook's help!"

Can you guess why Gemarakup needs an oven? For the solution, turn to page 92.

The Solutions

I. Lost on Skull Mountain

Gemarakup Finds the Way

Baruch turned tired but hopeful eyes to his friend. "What do you mean?" he asked.

"You gave me the idea, Baruch," Gemarakup answered, as he carefully picked over the items in the survival pack. "*Rosh Chodesh*. Don't you see?"

❦   ❦   ❦

In the times of the *Beis HaMikdash*, the Jews had to know when the new month began. Two witnesses who saw the first sliver of the new moon would make their way to the *Sanhedrin*, where they would be closely questioned. If their testimony was accepted, the *Sanhedrin* proclaimed a new month.

But how to let all of *Eretz Yisrael* know? Representatives of the *Sanhedrin* would ascend to the top of a mountain and light a fire. This fire would be seen by others far away, and they, too, would light fires — until all of Israel knew that the month had begun!

❦   ❦   ❦

"You've got matches here in your survival pack. Let's make a fire — a big one. I'm sure that the others are searching for us — we'll make it easy for them to find us!" The boys gathered twigs and taking care that the fire was contained and could not spread, they carefully set their blaze.

Half an hour later the search party, made up of several counselors and two forest rangers, found the two boys coughing over their smokey blaze. They were none the worse for their adventure; as a matter of fact, their friendship was much the better.

"Good idea, setting up a fire," one of the rangers complimented them. "Your camp can be very proud of the caution you took to avoid setting a forest fire. If not for your ingenuity it might have taken us all night to find you two."

Gemarakup smiled. "My friend's survival kit came in handy," he said.

"And *my* friend's brains, Baruch quickly countered. "Top-quality, the best that money can't buy," he added with a laugh.

II. The Momentous Mystery
of the Missing Money
Part 1
Tamar Proves Gemarakup's Innocence

"You know how Gemarakup uses stories to solve mysteries?" Tamar told her dumbfounded mother and blushing brother. "Well, this time *I've* solved the mystery — with a story!"

❦　❦　❦

It happened in Poland in the 1700's. Rabbi Tzvi Hirsch of Chortkov, a well-known *Rav*, discovered that the five hundred golden ducats that he'd saved up for his daughters' dowries had disappeared!

Only one man besides the *Rav* knew of the ducats' hiding place. That man was Asher Anschel, the *Rav*'s *shamash*, who had recently gotten married and opened a successful business in a nearby city. Though the *Rav* insisted that his faithful *shamash* was honest, the rest of the family suspected that he had made off with the money.

Finally, the *Rav* was forced to acquiesce to his family's demand that he confront the *shamash*. With a grim and pained look on his face, *Rav* Zvi Hirsch traveled to the nearby city and asked his *shamash* if he knew anything of the matter.

"I must confess, I took the ducats," Asher Anschel blurted out. "Only two hundred ducats remain. Here they are," he said, handing the astonished *Rav* a heavy bag. "I'll return the rest as soon as I can. Please forgive me."

The *Rav* returned to his city, disappointed in his *shamash* but satisfied that he and his family had not suspected him falsely. Not long afterwards, the constable in Chortkov, an honest and shrewd man, noticed one of the local peasantry, a man by the name of Carl, sitting in a tavern. This Carl, a poor man, merrily offered to buy a round of drinks for everyone in the bar. He paid with a golden ducat which, he explained, he'd found in the street.

When Carl repeated this generous gesture a second night, and a third, paying always with a golden ducat that "he'd found," the constable's suspicions were aroused. He walked over to the peasant and offered him cup after cup, until Carl was completely drunk. Then the constable confronted the peasant, demanding that he tell where he'd found the money.

"My wife worked for the Jew Rabbi," the drunken peasant confided, "and once, she saw where he'd hidden a whole load of golden coins."

A search of the peasant's home turned up the entire hoard, less three golden ducats spent on liquor. Proudly, the constable marched to the Rabbi's house to return the stolen money and share his triumph.

The *Rav* received the joyous news with consternation and dismay. His *shamash*! He raced to Asher Anschel's house to return the two hundred ducats and demand an explanation.

It was quite simple, explained Asher Anschel. "The *Rav* was very upset by his loss. Had I told the *Rav* I was innocent, you would have not had the money for the dowry. What are a few hundred ducats, compared to the *Rav*'s peace of mind? I felt it was worth hurting my reputation in order to save the Rav from worrying about the dowry." Asher Anschel concluded.

The *Rav* of Chortkov then blessed his *shamash*. "In the merit of this unselfish deed, may Hashem grant you much wealth, both for yourself and for generations to come," he said.

And sure enough, Asher Anschel became the founder of the world-renowned Rothschild dynasty, one of the wealthiest families the world has ever known!

🦋 🦋 🦋

Tamar turned to her brother. "Gemarakup, you told me that you knew the story of the Rothschild family. And just now you called yourself Baron Rothschild. Now admit it — your confession was the same as Asher Anschel's — not really a true one!"

Mrs. Finkel, whose cheeks had alternated between white and scarlet, turned to her son. Her voice was quiet and kind. "Yisrael David, tell me the truth. Did you, or did you not, take the money? And don't spare my feelings this time."

Gemarakup hung his head. "Imma, I don't want to make you feel bad. But of course I didn't take the money! I'm no thief!"

His mother enveloped her son in a warm hug. "No, you're just a sweet, misguided kid. When you will be a parent you will understand that as important as the money may seem to be, the thought that your child is, *chas v'shalom* a thief is a million times worse. *Baruch Hashem* I now know it wasn't you. And you," she said, kissing her daughter, "are a sister worthy of the world's greatest detective."

"But Imma," Gemarakup said after a moment, "if Tamar didn't take the money, and I didn't take the money — then who did?"

Who, indeed? For the answer to that mystery, turn to The Momentous Mystery of the Missing Money, Part 2, on page 21.

III. The Momentous Mystery
of the Missing Money
Part 2
Gemarakup Fingers the "Thief"

"Talking about *shidduchim* reminded me of a story my *rebbe* told me last week," Gemarakup told his avid listeners.

❧ ❧ ❧

There was once a poor tailor who came to the home of a revered *talmid chacham* for a loan.

Graciously, the *Rav* lent the tailor the money, and the two agreed that the loan would be repaid within a certain amount of time.

When that day came, the tailor duly made his way to the home of the *Rav*. He found him alone in his study, engrossed in a *sefer*. Not wanting to interrupt the great man's learning, the tailor merely took the money and placed it silently near the *Rav*.

So intent was the *Rav* on his books, though, that he took the money and, hardly aware of what he was doing, placed it in his *sefer*. The words of Torah took over his attention, and he completely forgot what he'd done. Later, he closed the *sefer* and replaced it on its shelf.

A few days passed. The *Rav*, realizing that the time for the debt's repayment had come and gone, sent for the tailor to ask him for the money.

"But I paid the *Rav* back in full," the tailor protested.

"I received no money from you," the *Rav* said gravely.

The matter eventually came to the *beis din*. Each man told his story; each remained adamant. The tailor insisted he'd paid back the loan, while the *Rav* countered that he'd received no money. The *beis din* finally came out with the verdict: The tailor must take a solemn vow that he had returned the money.

The *Rav* was aghast. Because of him, a Jew would swear falsely! He soon made up his mind: He wouldn't be the cause of such a grave sin. Instead, he renounced any claim to the money. And there, he felt, the matter came to an end.

But he was wrong. The matter did not rest there. Word of the case leaked out, and the townspeople, naturally, believed their beloved *Rav*. Incensed that someone would steal from him, they began to shun the tailor. His business dwindled away; soon he was forced to move to a hut on the outskirts of town, a scorned outcast.

Some time later, the *Rav* reached up for the *sefer* that he'd been studying on that fateful day. He opened it to the same page — and behold! There was the money that had been due him!

The *Rav* immediately realized that a terrible mistake had been made. Following the townspeople's directions, he swiftly made his way to the poorest part of town, to the tailor's dilapidated hut. "I see now what happened," the *Rav* said tearfully. "You paid me back, and I, hardly noticing, put the money into my *sefer*. I am so sorry."

" 'Sorry' doesn't restore my business and my good name," the tailor said bitterly.

"I will tell the townspeople all of what has transpired," the *Rav* promised.

"That will be of no use. They will simply say that you pity my fate and are lying in order to restore my reputation. They will say that you are a great *tzaddik* — and that I am a thief."

The *Rav* thought for a moment. Truly, it would be difficult to make amends.

Then he brightened. "I have a lovely daughter. She will be married to your son. No one will believe that I would allow my daughter to marry the son of a thief!"

And so it was.

❀ ❀ ❀

Gemarakup sniffed appreciatively. "Yum, I smell pecan-co-conut brownies." He strode quickly to the pile of cookbooks and picked up his mother's favorite. He skimmed the table of contents and opened up to a page. "But Imma, here's a secret ingredient that you left out." With a flourish, he held aloft two ten-dollar bills.

"Like the *Rav*, you were busy when you got the money. And, like the *Rav,* you put the money in the book without even noticing!"

Mrs. Finkel gave each of her children a hug. "Two detectives in one family! This calls for a celebration." She carefully opened the oven door. "Brownies, anyone?"

IV. Cracking the Case
of the Card Collection

Gemarakup Makes the Right Choice

Gemarakup led the two curious boys to the hallway near his classroom. "Wait here — and don't talk to each other," he commanded, as he entered the quiet room. "I'll be out in a minute."

In less than sixty seconds he returned. He pointed towards Yehoshua. "Come in. You," he added, looking at Dovid, "wait here for me."

Once inside, with the door carefully closed, Gemarakup pointed to a pile of *Rebbe* cards heaped on the teacher's desk. "Yehoshua, which cards are yours?" he asked.

The boy hardly favored the pile with a glance. "They're mine! All of them!"

Gemarakup nodded soberly. "Okay. Now, go out and send Dovid in."

With an uncertain glance, Yehoshua walked slowly out. Seconds later, it was Dovid's turn.

Gemarakup repeated the litany. "Dovid, which cards are yours?" he asked, pointing to the pile.

Dovid walked towards the desk. He fingered the cards, one by one, placing most of them in a pile. A few he put on the side.

He nodded towards the larger pile of cards. "Those are mine, for sure. The others, I don't think so, but I'm not certain."

Gemarakup walked over to the door. "Yehoshua, get in here," he commanded.

"You guys collect cards," he told them, when the two of them were standing together before him. "You'd do better to collect stories." Gemarakup whipped out a card. "This is the *Rav* of Lodz. Let me tell you a story about him":

❧ ❧ ❧

Two women in the town of Lodz shared a clothesline. One day, they got into an argument.

"The clothes hanging on the line are mine!" one of the women said.

"That's a lie! They belong to me!" the other insisted.

Finally, the two were brought to the wise *Rav* of Lodz. He heard the story, and then sent the two women out of his study. He turned to his wife. "Take some of our laundry and make a small mark on each piece, in a place where no one can see," he said to her.

Minutes later, he called in the first woman. "Is this your laundry?" he asked her.

She glanced at the basket. "Yes, it is all mine," she said.

Then he called in the second woman. "Is this your laundry?" he asked again.

The woman carefully looked through the basket, pulling out those items that belonged to the *Rav*. "These are not mine," she said, pointing to the small bundle.

The *Rav* then spoke to both women. "The laundry belongs to you," he said, pointing to the second woman. "Your honesty and care for other's property is clear from your careful examination of the laundry!"

❧ ❧ ❧

"Well, I took a hint from the *Rav* of Lodz, and had each of you check to see which cards were his. Dovid looked at every card and took the time to try and remember if it belonged to him. Yehoshua, you just wanted them all. Clearly, Dovid is much more careful about taking things that don't belong to him. Right?"

Yehoshua looked down, abashed. "I didn't mean to," he stammered. "It's just . . . first I really thought they were mine. And then, when I found my own cards in my backpack, Dovid just made me mad, and so I said . . ." His voice petered out.

Dovid made a threatening move in Yehoshua's direction, but Gemarakup checked him. "Hey, both of you were wrong. The *gedolim* in the cards were honest," he glanced at Yehoshua, "and patient and kind," he added, with a look at Dovid.

Both boys looked ashamed of themselves, and Gemarakup felt his sternness melt away. "C'mon guys, cheer up. After lunch tomorrow, you can both come to my house. I'll show you my collection."

"And maybe tell us some *gedolim* stories," Yehoshua asked quietly.

"No maybe about it," Gemarakup answered with a laugh.

V. When Is a Painter Not a Painter

Gemarakup Sees Beneath the Surface

"You really weren't very nice to Yossie," Tamar told her puzzled brother.

"What do you mean? What'd I do to Yossie? And what are you talking about hats for?"

Tamar smiled her favorite "annoy-my-brother" smile. "Let me tell you a story, smarty," she said.

❧ ❧ ❧

A great *rebbe* once decided to go on a journey anonymously. He donned the clothing of a poor wanderer and went off on his travels.

One Friday, he reached a certain town. As was the custom then, he stayed in *shul* after *davening* on Friday night, waiting to be invited by someone to join him for the *Shabbos* meal.

One by one, the more prosperous visitors to the town were invited. Finally, one of the wealthy townspeople nodded to the poor man and rather brusquely invited him to share his *Shabbos* meal.

During the course of the evening, though no one was openly rude or mean, the guest was not shown any warmth or real hospitality. He was placed at the end of the table, served last, and given whatever pieces were left over and unwanted by anyone else. When it came time to go to sleep, he was given an uncomfortable straw-filled pallet in one corner of a cold room.

After *Shabbos* the guest took his leave and was soon forgotten.

Not long afterwards exciting news stirred up the town. A great *rebbe* was expected for *Shabbos*. He would actually be joining them for a meal!

There was vast excitement because of the great honor. The *rebbe* came and was greeted by all the people of the town. The prosperous and important men of the town sat at the elaborately prepared table where the *rebbe* was to dine with them. They looked towards him, waiting expectantly for great words of Torah.

What they saw, though, surprised them. First, the *rebbe* dipped his finger into his beautifully carved silver goblet and carefully smeared wine upon his sleeve. Then he picked up the salt shaker and sprinkled his shoulder with salt. Finally, the astonished townspeople watched him take the crisp piece of chicken that had been placed before him and neatly put it on his lap!

After a shocked silence, one of the amazed townspeople found the courage to ask the *rebbe* for an explanation of his strange behavior.

"The answer is quite simple," the *rebbe* replied. "When I was here some time ago, I was honored with none of this beautiful hospitality. And yet I have not changed at all; I am the same man who appeared to you in the guise of a poor man. Only one thing has changed: my clothing. The hospitality that you are offering me here is clearly not for me, it is for my clothes. Therefore, I am feeding my clothing and not myself!"

❦ ❦ ❦

"You were really anxious to get Yossie Fein to learn with you," Tamar said. "Yet, when that same Yossie Fein asked you if you wanted his help, you very rudely turned him down."

"Huh?" Gemarakup was still bewildered.

"The painter, Gemarakup! Who do you think was painting this house? It was Yossie, whom you would have realized if only you would have been decent enough to look at him. But he was dressed in messy overalls and so you figured you were better than he was and that he couldn't possibly teach you a thing! But when he puts on a hat and a suit — then you can talk with him and learn with him and treat him like a human being!"

Gemarakup, his cheeks as red as Tamar's apple, looked at his father. "Yossie . . . the painter?" he blurted out.

Mr. Finkel nodded his head with a small smile. "That's right, Yisrael David."

"Abba, may I be excused from the table," Gemarakup said

quietly. "There's something I have to take care of in the kitchen. An apology."

"Before you do, Gemarakup, maybe you should take the hat off," his father said gently.

"You can hang it up near the overalls," Tamar added with a wicked smile.

VI. Of Cabbages and Rings

Gemarakup Finds the Missing Ring

"I think I know where the ring is," Gemarakup told his bemused mother, as he feverishly grabbed one cookie after another and broke each into two. "I figured it out from a story I was reading about Syrian Jews".

❧ ❧ ❧

A good Jew by the name of Shimon De Fejuto lived in Aleppo, Syria, many years ago. This Shimon was once approached by an Arab, who asked him for a loan of two hundred golden coins.

"I only loan money on two conditions," Shimon told the Arab. "You must sign a note admitting that you owe the money and will pay me back in six months. And you must bring someone as a guarantor that the loan will be repaid."

The Arab smiled slyly. "I will gladly sign the note," he told Shimon. "And as for a guarantor — you believe in God, do you not? Let your God be the guarantor then. You do trust Him, don't you?"

Shimon did trust *Hashem* — though he didn't trust the Arab. But, not wanting to make a *chilul Hashem*, Shimon agreed to the strange condition. He wrapped up two hundred golden coins in a red scarf and handed them to the Arab.

On his way home, the Arab stopped at one of his fields. It was the harvest season, and workers were picking heads of cabbage. The Arab noticed some of the workers slacking. Enraged, he walked over and began to berate them for their laziness. He was so angry that he hardly noticed that he had put the red scarf down on the ground. Nor did he remember when he walked away, leaving the scarf behind.

When he returned home he realized what he had done. He rushed back to the fields but could find no trace of his money.

The next morning, Shimon's wife sent a servant out to the market. He returned with three large heads of cabbage. As she began to cut one apart, she found, to her astonishment, a red scarf full of golden coins! She called her husband, who smiled and took the money.

Six months later, the Arab shamefacedly returned to Shimon's home. "I cannot repay the loan," he admitted. "The money was lost."

Shimon smiled. "Have no fear," he said, as he pulled out the red scarf. "Your Guarantor has repaid me."

🦋   🦋   🦋

"When I heard you talking about stuffed cabbage I remembered this story. Now, I don't think your ring is in a cabbage. But it could be hidden in a different food — in one of the fortune cookies! And yes — here it is!"

From out of a golden cookie came the shiny golden ring!

As his mother hugged him happily, Gemarakup grinned. "The fortune said my search would be rewarded!" he laughed.

His mother laughed with him. "And so it is! I can't serve these broken cookies to anyone. Call Tamar down and pour yourself a glass of chocolate milk. We're going to celebrate!"

VII. The New Kid in Town

Gemarakup Solves the Dilemma

Sasha quietly followed Gemarakup back into the Finkel home. "Call your parents," Gemarakup commanded, after a hurried conference with his mother, "and tell them you're staying for supper. My father will drive you back afterwards.

"And now," he continued, walking up the stairs towards his bedroom, "I want to tell you a story. Our talk about Choni HaMa'agal and the rain in *Eretz Yisrael* made me think of it."

☙ ☙ ☙

Abba Chilkiya was a grandson of Choni HaMa'agal. Like his grandfather before him, Abba Chilkiya was the one to whom the nation turned during times of drought.

Once, during a particularly dry year, the Sages sent two messengers to ask Abba Chilkiya to pray for rain. They went to his house, but he was not there. They then went to the fields and found him working there. They greeted him politely, but he did not even turn his face to them to say hello.

As evening came on, he turned homeward. To the great astonishment of the messengers, he walked barefoot, only putting on his shoes when he came to a river that he had to ford. Whenever he passed by thorn bushes, he would raise his protective garments.

He and his wife sat down to dinner. He whispered to her, "I know that these men are here to ask me to pray for rain. Come, let us go upstairs to pray, and if Hashem grants our wish the men will not know that it is due to our *tefillos.*"

The two walked up to the roof, each *davening.* And shortly thereafter, the sky grew cloudy and the rains came down.

The messengers, undeceived by Abba Chilkiya's ruse, told him, "We know, Master, that it is in your merit that the rain comes. But tell us, why was it that you did not greet us when we first saw you?"

"Because I was hired as a day laborer, and I dared not waste my employer's time," Abba Chilkiya explained.

"And why did you walk without shoes, except when you went into the water?"

"As I walked on earth I could be careful of what I was stepping on," Abba Chilkiya explained, "but in the water I cannot see what is beneath me, and so need shoes."

"And why did you raise your garments just when you walked through thorns, when it was most needed?"

"Because," said Abba Chilkiya, "if my skin is scratched it will quickly heal. But if my garment tears, I cannot replace it."

❧ ❧ ❧

"The story goes on," Gemarakup told a watchful Sasha, "and shows how Abba Chilkiya's behavior, which seemed so strange, was really very logical.

"I always liked the story," Gemarakup continued, "but the part about him letting himself be scratched, rather than tear his clothing, seemed to me a bit — unrealistic. Until now."

Gemarakup put his hands in his pocket, hesitated for a moment, then spoke again. "I don't want to embarrass you, Sash, but I'm wondering if you're staying out of our game —

and out of our recess — because, like Abba Chilkiya, you're worried about your clothing."

Sasha flushed and nodded. "My parents didn't have much in Russia," he explained. "Once they became *Shomer Shabbos* they both lost their jobs. They had no savings, no property. Nothing. And now that we're here, my father is learning. He wants to make up for the years he lost growing up in the Soviet Union. I . . . I'm very proud of him," he said, rather defiantly.

Gemarakup's eyes sparkled. "You should be. He's a hero!"

"Yes, a hero without much money. I have . . . this one pair of pants for school, and another for Shabbos. I don't really mind. We've got enough to eat, after all. We're happy here. But if I join the guys outside at recess, I'll be filthy, like you are. I can't do it, not with one pair of pants. You see that, don't you?"

Gemarakup nodded slowly. "Sasha, I need your help," he said, after a short pause.

"*My* help?"

"Yeah. See that mess over there that used to be a closet? My mom has been after me for weeks to clean it out. If you can spare a few minutes, I'd like to go through all the clothes. Half the stuff in there doesn't fit me anymore. Imma wanted to send it to *Eretz Yisrael,* but if you know someone closer, that's just a bit shorter than me," he grinned and favored Sasha with a long glance, "you'd be doing me a big favor taking the stuff off my hands."

Sasha hesitated, then laughed. "A big favor, huh?"

"You bet. And Sasha . . ."

"Yes?"

"Tomorrow, I'll give you some batting pointers. Okay?"

"Sure, Gemarakup."

VIII. Gemarakup and the Great Purim Caper

Gemarakup Unmasks the Truth

O'Rourke looked at Gemarakup, astonished. Then his face creased into a broad smile. "Let me guess, kid. You must be Gemarakup."

Gemarakup nodded, his grin as wide as O'Rourke's own.

"They told me to be careful of you, that you were the most likely to see through us. I guess they were right."

Before Gemarakup's friends could recover from one shock, they were faced with still another. O'Rourke walked towards the back of the van and opened the door. "You can come out now. We've been found out!"

Out of the van stepped one black-suited figure after another: Slugger's father, Mr. Finkel, Chaim Cohen's dad, and even — could it be — Rabbi Eliach, the boys' *rebbe*!

O'Rourke looked at the boys' bewildered faces and laughed. "Happy Purim, guys! Your dads decided that if you insisted on being hoods on Purim — you'd get the royal treatment."

Mr. Finkel interrupted with a grin. "That's right. Let me introduce you kids to my old friend Danny Schwartz. Danny runs a security agency, and he offered to lend me his van, siren and all, for our little *Purim shpiel*. And these two tough characters —" at this, the uniformed policemen took sheepish bows — "are Nachum Singer and Avi Marks, two fellows who enjoy a little fun on Purim, and offered their services."

O'Rourke shook his head. "We had it all down pat. But you ruined the surprise, Gemarakup. How'd you do it?"

Gemarakup laughed. "It reminded me of a story, of course."

❧ ❧ ❧

In addition to being a genius and *gadol b'Torah*, the *Rambam*, Rabbi Moshe ben Maimon, was also an incredibly gifted doctor. The ruling sultan, aware of the *Rambam's* incomparable healing skills, decided to make him his personal physician.

But as always, when a Jew succeeds, there are enemies who grow jealous. A non-Jewish physician, seeing the *Rambam's* fame and honor, approached the sultan.

"If your doctor is truly a great healer, he will cure this poor unfortunate man whom I bring before you," the non-Jew told the Sultan. "He has been blind since his birth."

The *Rambam,* sensing a trap, shook his head. "I am no miracle worker," he declared. "I cannot cure one such as this."

"And yet," the non-Jew announced, "I can!"

With that, he took out a vial and placed a few drops of medicine in each of the poor man's eyes.

The blind man blinked and looked around in wonder. "I can see! I can see!" he shouted, walking deftly around the room in order to prove that his vision had returned.

The *Rambam* looked wisely at the Sultan. "Your Majesty," he said, "I wish to make certain that the cure has indeed worked properly. May I?"

The ruler nodded his assent. The *Rambam* took two different colored cloths, one in each hand. "Tell me, blind man, what colors do you see?"

The man looked straight at the cloths. "The one on that side," he said, pointing to the right, "is red; the other, yellow."

"A miracle!" the sultan murmured, for the blind man had been absolutely right.

"Not a miracle. A fraud!" shouted the *Rambam*. "For if this man has been blind from birth, if he has never seen a color before — tell me, then, how could he know how to name the colors correctly?!"

❧   ❧   ❧

"I also began to suspect a hoax," Gemarakup continued. "After all, O'Rourke wasn't exactly knowledgeable about *Yiddishkeit*. He didn't even know what Purim was. And yet, if he had never learned a thing about Judaism, how was it that he knew to open my *siddur* to the first page, to *Modeh Ani*? Anyone else would have opened it from the back, the way an English book is opened.

"No, it was clear that, like the blind man, this police officer knew a lot more than he was admitting. When I put that together with the fact that it was Purim — I knew we were being fooled!

"And now," he concluded, "I'd appreciate if O'Rourke — that is Mr. Schwartz — could give me a ride home. I want to get out of these clothes as fast as I can — before I get arrested again!"

IX. The Rebbe's Mystery

Gemarakup Learns His Lesson

"Okay, Gemarakup, looks like you've figured it out. Why not tell the rest of the class what I was doing this morning?" Rabbi Eliach said, smiling.

Gemarakup turned to his bewildered classmates. "You all heard the story we learned this morning in *Gemara shiur*":

❀ ❀ ❀

Rabbi Akiva's students were learning a difficult matter and finding it hard to concentrate. So Rabbi Akiva, in order to awaken them and get them thinking again, told them a fascinating *vort* connecting the 127 lands that Queen Esther reigned over, with the 127 years that *Sarah Imeinu* lived.

❀ ❀ ❀

"My theory is that the *Rebbe* followed Rabbi Akiva's lead. Rabbi Eliach also wanted to wake up his students — and he did it, not with a *vort,* but with a mystery!"

Rabbi Eliach nodded. "Quite right, Yisrael David. Like Rabbi Akiva's students, I thought you needed something to help wake you up a bit."

Gemarakup looked at his smiling teacher. "But *Rebbe,* it's not really fair. You said you were solving a mystery with a story, not using a teaching trick!"

Rabbi Eliach grinned. "And I was, Gemarakup, I sure was. What harder mystery is there to solve — than the mystery of how to make sixth-graders listen to *dikduk* lessons!"

X. A Graffiti Getaway

Gemarakup Uncovers the Hiding Place

"We've checked there already," Uncle Ezra objected, as his nephew turned towards the small wooden door that led out to the overgrown garden.

Gemarakup ignored his protests and, followed by the others, made his way outside.

The garden was dark and forbidding. Gemarakup carefully picked his way through weeds and broken bottles, his eyes scanning the ivy-covered walls of the *shul*. Finally, he found what he was looking for: a rusted drainpipe.

"Before I uncover the criminal, let me tell you a story," Gemarakup told the bemused adults surrounding him.

❈ ❈ ❈

Thousands of years ago there lived a man who wished for nothing except to learn Torah from the lips of the Sages. But he was poor, terribly poor, and in those days in order to attend *shiurim* a person had to pay an entrance fee at the door to the *beis medrash*. Though the man begged and pleaded, the watchman at the door was adamant: without the admission fee, the man could not enter.

The weather outside was freezing and blustery; inside the *beis medrash*, though, it was warm with the fire of Torah learning. The great Sage spoke, the others listened and argued and questioned and learned.

After a while, though, the Sage realized that the light was growing dim. He looked upwards at the skylight in the roof and saw a shadowy figure. The people investigated and, to their horror, discovered a man frozen to the roof!

The poor man, determined to hear words of Torah, had sat quietly on the roof, drinking in the Sage's wisdom and slowly almost froze to death!

When the man had recovered from his ordeal, the Sage announced that due to the man's incredible dedication, he would henceforth be an honored pupil with a place in the *beis medrash*.

The poor man's name was Hillel, and he was destined to become one of the greatest leaders of *klal Yisrael*.

❦ ❦ ❦

"When I saw the skylight I remembered this story, and I realized that if the hoodlum isn't inside the *shul* — he must be on top of it! And I'll bet he used this drainpipe to get there!"

At once the policemen were shinnying up the pipe — and in less time than it takes to say "Gemarakup does it again!" they returned, with a sullen graffiti artist firmly in their grip.

"Good going," Uncle Ezra complimented his nephew, as they re-entered the *shul*. "And now, I suppose it's too late to get the *sefarim* packed up."

Mr. Finkel smiled. "No, let's finish what we started," he laughed. "After all, I'm used to waiting for you, Ezra. And when it comes to getting pizza — we have the patience of Hillel!"

XI. Gemarakup Cracks the Code

Gemarakup Discovers the Secret

"In *shiur* today, the *rebbe* talked about some of the laws of writing on *Shabbos*," Gemarakup explained, as he lined up before the portable outdoor oven for his cup of cocoa. "I was particularly interested in one unusual case":

❦ ❦ ❦

It happened during a dangerous time for the Jews. The *Rabbonim* had to send messages to each other but they were afraid that they would fall into the wrong hands and endanger the sender. So they came up with a scheme: They wrote the message using a substance which was invisible. Only when the paper was dipped into another substance, would the message become clear.

❧   ❧   ❧

"The Gemara talks about whether or not one may add this ingredient to paper, in order to bring out the invisible writing, on *Shabbos*. But since today is Monday, we've got no problem at all.

"You told me that your friend Shuey is very bright. Too bright to make a mistake like sending a blank paper. I looked closely at the paper and saw wet marks on it. My theory is that Shuey used today's equivalent of invisible ink to send you a message. You may not know this, but if you write something using lemon juice as your 'ink,' the letters do not come out on the paper until you hold the paper up to steam. So," Gemarakup ended, "let's do that right now."

As he dangled the paper over the large vat of steaming cocoa, letters soon appeared.

"You'll never figure this one out," Shuey had written.

Pinchas took a sip of the cocoa and smiled. "He's right, you know. I would *never* have figured it out. But he didn't count on my friend, Gemarakup!"

Glossary

Abba: father

Aron Kodesh: Holy Ark in which Torah scrolls are kept

ba'alei teshuvah (pl.)*:* returnee to Torah observance

Bais Hamikdash: the Holy Temple

Baruch Hashem: Thank God

Beis Din: Jewish Court

beis medrash: study hall

benching (Yid.)*:* reciting Grace After Meals

chasunah: wedding

chas v'shalom: God forbid

chesed: kindness

chevrah: group

chilul Hashem: desecration of the name of God.

Chumash: Pentateuch; Five Books of Moses

chutzpah: insolence, lack of respect

davening (Yid.)*:* praying

dikduk: grammar

Eretz Yisrael: Land of Israel

erev Shabbos: Sabbath eve

gabbai: synagogue official

gadol (pl. *gedolim*)*:* Torah leader of the generation

Gemara: that portion of the Talmud which discusses the *Mishnah;* loosely a synonym for the Talmud as a whole

gematria: use of letters as numerals

genizah: storage place for Torah Scrolls, *tefillin, mezuzos* and *seforim* that cannot be used

golem: legendary automaton of clay

halachos (singular: *halachah*): Torah laws

Imma: mother

Klal Yisrael: the Jewish People

lashon hara: gossip, slanderous talk

midrashim (singular: *midrash*): classical anthology of the Sage's homiletical teachings on the Torah.

minhag: custom

minyan: quorum of ten men necessary for conducting a prayer service

Mishnah: the teaching of the *Tannaim* * which form the basis of the Talmud

netz: sunrise

nosh: snacks

parashah: Torah portion

p'shat: the simple explanation of a Torah or Talmudic text

Purim: Holiday celebrating the rescue of the Jews in Persia from the decree of the wicked Haman as recorded in the Book of *Esther.*

Rav: rabbi

rebbe: teacher of Torah

Rosh Chodesh: the beginning of a Jewish month

Sanhedrin: Supreme Rabbinic Court in the times of the Holy Temple comprised of 71 judges.

sefer (pl. *sefarim*): book of Torah subject

seudah: festive meal (Purim Seudah — one of the four *mitzvos* of Purim)

shalach monos: one of the four *mitzvos* of Purim — gift of food sent to friends and neighbors

Shamash: (a) synagogue caretaker; (b) rabbi's assistant or personal secretary *sheker:* lie

shidduch: matrimonial match

shiur (pl. *shiurim*): lesson, especially a Torah lesson

shlepping (Yid.): drag or carry

Shlomo HaMelech: King Solomon

Shomer Shabbos: Sabbath observer

shtender: movable lectern

shul (Yid): synagogue

sugya (Aramaic): a passage or debate on a given topic in the Talmud

talmid chacham: Torah scholar

Tanach: the Bible — initials of names of the three parts; the Torah, the Prophets, the Writings

Tanna (pl. *Tannaim*): an authority cited in the Mishnah

tefillos (singular: *tefillah*): prayers

tzaddik (pl. *tzaddikim*): righteous, saintly person

vort (Yid.): a discourse on a Torah subject

yahrzeit (Yid.): the anniversary of a person's death

Yiddishkeit (Yid.): Judaism